Let's Explore a

Pirate Ship

L | HAMMOND World Atlas
Part of the Langenscheidt Publishing Group

Published in the United States and its territories and Canada by
HAMMOND WORLD ATLAS CORPORATION
Part of the Langenscheidt Publishing Group
36-36 33rd Street
Long Island City, NY 11106

Created and produced by
Nicholas Harris, Sarah Hartley
and Erica Williams, Orpheus Books Ltd.

Text Nicholas Harris

Illustrator Brian Lee

Cover design: Jeff Beebe

Printed and bound in Malaysia
Tien Wah Press (Pte.) Ltd.
Singapore
October 2009

ISBN-13: 978-0843-713787

Let's Explore a
Pirate Ship

Nicholas Harris

Illustrated by Brian Lee

HAMMOND World Atlas
Part of the Langenscheidt Publishing Group

LIFE ABOARD A PIRATE SHIP

The ship's crew was made up of sailors who turned to a life of piracy to escape the rough treatment they received on **merchant ships** or warships. There, they lived on rotten food and frequently suffered disease and injury.

The captain of those ships often handed out harsh punishments.

But life at sea was tough on a pirate ship too. The men lived in cramped conditions, sleeping among rats and eating a poor diet. There were no doctors to tend to the sick or wounded.

1 Ship's wheel The ship was steered by a **helmsman**, using a wheel.

2 Mainmast The tallest mast of the ship.

3 Great cabin The captain used this as a dining room, a map room, and a place to entertain.

4 Rigging The sails, together with the ropes used to control them.

5 Capstan A winding machine used for raising or lowering the anchor. Sailors pushed levers, called handspikes, to turn the capstan.

6 Cannon A gun mounted on a wheeled carriage. It fired cannonballs at enemy ships.

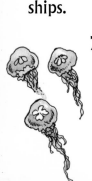

7 Crew's quarters Most sailors slept in hammocks slung from the ceilings.

SPANISH GALLEON

Christopher Columbus, in the service of Spain, first landed in the Americas in 1492. Spanish seamen began to explore the "New World," beginning with the Caribbean Sea and moving on to the mainland—what became known as the **"Spanish Main."** Spain claimed much of Central and South America as its own. The Spanish conquered the great empires of two native peoples, the **Aztecs** and the **Incas,** stole their vast stocks of gold and silver, and shipped them back to Spain.

The ships the Spanish used to carry their treasure were called galleons. These warships were sometimes more than 115 feet (35 meters) long and 33 feet (10 meters) wide. They had up to 60 cannon and a crew of more than 200 men. Despite their great size and weaponry, the galleons were often out-maneuvered by the smaller, faster pirate ships.

Pirates would often take a treasure ship by surprise, swapping a friendly flag for the Jolly Roger moments before their attack. The sight of the skull and crossbones or crossed swords would often terrify the crew of the galleon into surrender without a fight.

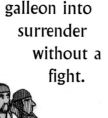

Yet pirates were treated better and had more freedoms than "normal" sailors. Both the captain and the **quartermaster** were elected by the crew. This made them trusted men rather than hated **figures** of authority.

Many pirate crews made up their own rules, which they agreed to follow. They shared what they looted between them. If a pirate was found guilty of stealing, or was judged a coward in battle, he was **marooned** on a remote island.

8 Tiller A lever attached to the rudder.

9 Bilge pumps These drained the **bilges**, the lowest part of the ship, which usually filled up with smelly water.

10 Galley The cabin where the cooking was done. The hearth is enclosed in bricks to keep in the heat.

11 Rudder A large wooden paddle fitted to the stern (back) of the ship.

12 Ship's stores The ship carried food stores, (biscuit, grain, and salted meat) water and beer, gunpowder, cannonballs, spare sails, and ropes.

13 Ballast Heavy rocks in the bilges helped keep the ship stable.

Several men were needed to fire a cannon. First, a loader packed gunpowder into the barrel, followed by the ball. A sponger used a long stick called a rammer to push both powder and ball down the barrel. The gun crew hauled on ropes to pull the cannon to the gunport. The gunner held a burning wick to a hole at the end of the gun, lighting the gunpowder.

Both galleon and the pirate ship relied heavily on the wind. By adjusting the position of the sails, the ship could change its speed and direction. The sails were attached to the masts by horizontal beams called **yards**. Ropes called lifts held them in place. Other ropes, known as **halyards**, hoisted the sails into position. The crew climbed up and down the rigging on rope ladders called **ratlines** in order to reach the sails and the **crow's nest**.

Faced with a pirate attack, a galleon's captain would sometimes turn and fight, firing a cannon directly at the bow of the pirate ship. A lucky shot could shatter her **hull**. This was called raking.

INTO BATTLE

A pirate ship was normally met with little resistance. Pirate crews often outnumbered the crew of a galleon. Faced with the challenge of pirates wielding razor-sharp swords, few galleon crews dared to put up a fight. But sometimes, especially if there were trained guards aboard the galleon, a fierce fight began. Following an initial bombardment by cannon fire, the pirate ship would pull alongside the galleon. The pirates used **grappling irons** to pull the two ships together . . .

As long as people have sailed across the seas, there have been pirates. Some were out to steal all they could for themselves. Others, called **privateers**, were employed in the service of their country. Their kings gave them authority to plunder foreign ships in exchange for a share of what they took. Many privateers became pirates when their countries made peace.

Runaway **slaves**, adventurers, and **outlaws** also became pirates. Some, like the inhabitants of the Spanish island of Hispaniola, turned to piracy after being forced off their land. They were called "**buccaneers**" after the *boucan* barbecues on which they smoked their meat. When war between Britain and Spain came to an end in 1714, privateers and buccaneers joined forces. The Golden Age of Piracy had begun.

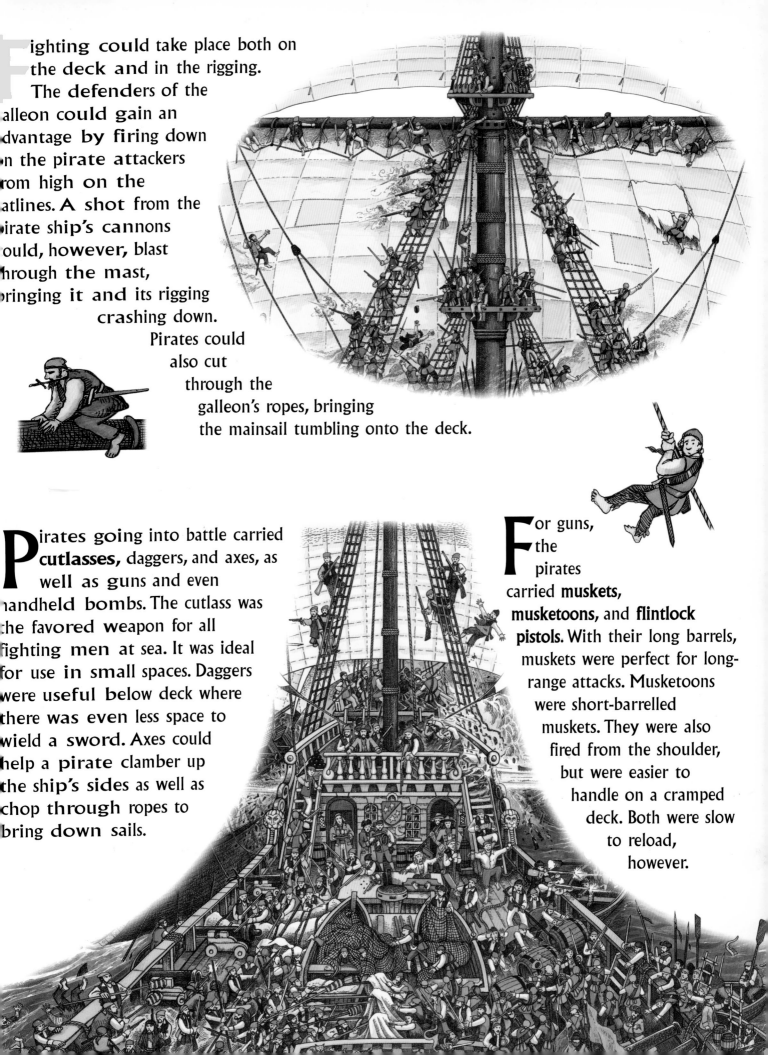

Fighting could take place both on the deck and in the rigging.

The defenders of the galleon could gain an advantage by firing down on the pirate attackers from high on the ratlines. A shot from the pirate ship's cannons could, however, blast through the mast, bringing it and its rigging crashing down. Pirates could also cut through the galleon's ropes, bringing the mainsail tumbling onto the deck.

Pirates going into battle carried **cutlasses,** daggers, and axes, as well as guns and even handheld bombs. The cutlass was the favored weapon for all fighting men at sea. It was ideal for use in small spaces. Daggers were useful below deck where there was even less space to wield a sword. Axes could help a pirate clamber up the ship's sides as well as chop through ropes to bring down sails.

For guns, the pirates carried **muskets, musketoons,** and **flintlock pistols.** With their long barrels, muskets were perfect for long-range attacks. Musketoons were short-barrelled muskets. They were also fired from the shoulder, but were easier to handle on a cramped deck. Both were slow to reload, however.

UNDER THE SEA

An 18th-century ship could be wrecked in a number of ways, besides being sunk in battle. A ship could become top-heavy due to badly loaded cargo. This could make it topple over in the wind. Storms such as **hurricanes**, which caused high winds and massive waves, were an ever-constant threat. Sharp **coral reefs** or rocks just below the water's surface could smash a hole in a ship's hull, causing water to flood in. Sometimes, shipwrecked sailors could make their escape in rowboats or on rafts. But many drowned for one simple reason—very few sailors could swim!

When a wooden ship sunk, water currents washed silt, sand, and mud from the sea bed into the ship's hull. There, where there was no oxygen to rot away the wood, the timbers might remain preserved for centuries afterwards. But any wood left uncovered would be gradually eaten away by tiny marine creatures. The weakened timbers eventually collapsed and rotted away.

Over the years, the wreck would gradually become part of a coral reef. Reefs are built up by tiny animals that live in the warm, shallow seas of the tropics. The corals group together to become colonies and make hard cases around their bodies. Eventually, brightly colored shapes appear. Many other sea creatures, including fish, clams, and starfish live among the coral.

When a Spanish treasure ship sank in the Caribbean, its cargo might go down with it. This cargo often included valuable coins of gold and silver such as "doubloons" and "pesos." The name doubloon comes from the Spanish word for double. These coins were worth twice that of another gold coin called the "pistole." Pesos were silver coins that were stamped with an "8" to mark their value. That's why pirates called them **"pieces of eight."** Pirates divided up treasure more or less equally between them, although the captain received a little more than the others.

If a treasure ship went down in shallow water, it would be possible to **salvage** it. People can only hold their breath underwater for a few minutes at most, so divers on a salvage operation had to work fast. Heavy items like cannon and chests required ropes and grappling irons to lift them. They could be pulled to the surface from a salvage ship anchored above the wreck.

GLOSSARY

Aztec A member of a powerful empire in Mexico conquered by the Spanish in the early 16th century.

ballast Stones packed into the bottom of a ship to keep the ship upright, especially in rough weather.

bilges The lowest part of the ship, where ballast is placed.

buccaneers Former hunters who turned to piracy after being driven from their home island, Hispaniola, by the Spanish.

capstan A winding machine used for raising or lowering the anchor.

cargo The goods carried on board a ship.

coral reef An undersea bank made up of the skeletons of many thousands of tiny animals, called coral polyps.

crow's nest A lookout platform around a ship's mast.

cutlass A sword with a short, broad blade.

flintlock pistol A light pistol. When the trigger was pulled, a piece of flint was struck, producing sparks that ignited gunpowder.

galleon A large sailing ship used in warfare and trading between the 15th and 18th centuries.

grappling iron A hook with several prongs, attached to a rope and used for holding on to or lifting objects, or to secure two ships together.

halyard A rope used for hoisting a ship's sails into position.

helmsman The sailor who steers the ship.

hull The main outer body of the ship.

hurricane A large rotating storm with high winds that forms over tropical seas, such as the Caribbean Sea and Gulf of Mexico.

Inca A member of a powerful empire in Peru conquered by the Spanish in the 16th century.

Jolly Roger The flag flown by pirate ships.

marooning A punishment for a pirate who broke the ship's rules. He was left alone on a remote island with very little food or water.

merchant ship A ship that carries cargo that is for sale.

musket A gun with a long barrel, similar to a rifle, used between the 16th and 18th centuries.

musketoon A shorter version of the musket, popular with pirates.

outlaw A criminal on the run.

pieces of eight The pirate name for Spanish silver coins.

privateer Someone given permission by the government of one country to attack ships belonging to another. The name was short for "private men-of-war."

quartermaster The crew member in charge of food and living conditions on board a ship.

ratlines Rope ladders fixed to the rigging that enable sailors to climb up to the sails.

rigging The ship's sails and the ropes used to control them.

salvage To retrieve the contents of a shipwreck.

slaves People that were forced to work for other people, who "owned" them.

Spanish Main The Caribbean coast of Central and South America, claimed by Spain.

yard The pole on a mast that carries a sail.